SABAN'S

MIGHTY MORPHIN POWER RANGERS™

PAPERCUTZ™

SABAN'S

MIGHTY MORPHIN POWER RANGERS™

① "RITA REPULSA'S ATTITUDE ADJUSTMENT"

Stefan Petrucha – Writer
PH Marcondes – Artist
Laurie E. Smith– Colorist

MIGHTY MORPHIN POWER RANGERS #1
"Rita Repulsa's Attitude Adjustment"

STEFAN PETRUCHA – Writer
PH MARCONDES – Artist
LAURIE E. SMITH – Colorist
BRYAN SENKA – Letterer

UMESH PATEL (RANGER CREW) – Special Thanks
KAY OLIVER, MARY RAFFERTY, GREG SANTOS – Extra Special Thanks
BETH SCORZATO – Production Coordinator
MICHAEL PETRANEK – Editor
JIM SALICRUP
Editor-in-Chief

ISBN: 978-1-59707-696-8 paperback edition
ISBN: 978-1-59707-697-5 hardcover edition

Printed in China
April 2014 by New Era Printing LTD
Unit C, 8/F Worldwide Centre
123 Chung Tau Street, Hong Kong

Papercutz books may be purchased for business or promotional use. For information on bulk purchases please contact
Macmillan Corporate and Premium Sales Department at (800) 221-7945 x5442.

Distributed by Macmillan

First Printing

After 10,000 years of imprisonment, the evil sorceress Rita Repulsa and her loyal minions have been freed from their space dumpster, when astronauts on a routine mission accidentally opened it on the moon. Enraged, Rita decided to conquer the nearest planet-- Earth. But her arch nemesis, the heroic sage Zordon, has been patiently waiting for this day.

With the assistance of his wisecracking robotic sidekick Alpha-5, Zordon recruits 5 "teenagers with attitude"-- Jason, Kimberly, Billy, Trini, and Zack-- to receive superpowers beyond their wildest dreams and defend the Earth as the Mighty Morphin Power Rangers. Aided by giant robotic vehicles modeled after dinosaurs called "Zords," the Power Rangers fight back the evil alien hordes of Rita Repulsa.

Jason is a black belt in karate and the leader of the Power Rangers. His martial arts are his passion and he spends much of his free time training, both learning new moves and perfecting old ones. When he's not training Jason is working on his schoolwork or hanging out with friends, like most other seventeen-year-old guys.

Jason is loyal and patriotic. He loves being a Power Ranger and takes his duty to save the world very seriously. But he's still a teen first and foremost, with all the trials and tribulations that entails. Jason isn't always the most outspoken guy, preferring to keep his feelings to himself, and letting his hands and feet do the talking while fighting with the Power Rangers. But even with his rough exterior, his sly smile can reveal the mischievous boy-next-door he is at heart.

Jason draws power from the Tyrannosaurus rex. His weapon is the Power Sword, and he pilots the Megazord when it is fully assembled.

Weapon:
Power Sword

Zord:
Tyrannosaurus
Dinozord

Notes:
Jason was a martial arts
instructor at Ernie's Juice Bar
and Gym

THE PINK RANGER (KIMBERLY HART)

Kimberly is a bright and beautiful girl who loves shopping and gymnastics. She's the most popular girl at school and loves the attention of the limelight. But beneath her bubbly exterior she's fiercely independent and has always longed for adventure and danger. Kimberly is always upbeat with her friends, but she's got a wicked streak of sarcasm and one-liners that she saves for the bad guys.

Kimberly is also a champion gymnast, and she brings these skills to her work with the Power Rangers. She trains hard not just to compete, but also to be able to jump and flip her way out of almost any situation. With the Power Rangers, Kimberly draws power from the Pterodactyl and her weapon is the Power Bow.

Weapon:
Power Bow

Zord:
Pterodactyl
Dinozord

Notes:
Local bully Skull has a big crush on her.

MIGHTY MORPHIN POWER RANGERS

THE BLUE RANGER (BILLY CRANSTON)

Billy is super-smart and this can sometimes get in the way of him communicating with other kids. But once they get to know him they realize that he's more than just a nerd. Billy is sweet and kind-hearted, on top of being a super-genius. He focuses all his energy on his academics and often talks in techno-speak, using complicated language that confuses most people. Lucky for him, Trini always seems to understand.

Billy always wants to know how everything works and is constantly studying the world around him. His greatest hobby is learning. In spite of his intelligence, Billy is usually shy and reserved, except for with his friends, the other Power Rangers. With them he feels like he can truly be himself.

As a Power Ranger, Billy draws power from the Triceratops and his weapon is the Power Lance.

Weapon:
  Power Lance

Zord:
  Triceratops
  Dinozord

Notes:
  Billy built the Power Ranger communicators.

THE YELLOW RANGER (TRINI KWAN)

Trini has been described by Zordon himself as the one with "lightning hands and a peaceful soul." She is deeply dedicated to her martial arts practice, constantly working on both the spiritual and physical aspects of her karate. Trini is highly observant and highly intelligent, which makes her the only person who truly understands Billy. At school, Trini is active in lots of activities and causes and is a role model for other students.

Even with her extraordinary gifts, she is very patient and slow to anger. But, if pushed, she will shut down any threat with little effort. When her training takes over, she is a razor-sharp fighter with lightning reflexes.

With the Power Rangers, Trini draws power from the Sabertooth Tiger, and her weapon is the Power Daggers.

Weapon:
Power Daggers

Zord:
Sabertooth
Tiger
Dinozord

Notes:
Trini has a secret fear of heights.

THE BLACK RANGER (ZACK TAYLOR)

Zack loves life and always lives to the fullest. He makes friends with everyone and can always light up the room with his personality. He's got a good heart and a seemingly boundless supply of energy. Smooth talking and street-smart, he can often disarm his opponents with a quick smile and his wit. He also fancies himself quite the ladies' man. At school, Zack can often be found hanging around the music rooms, telling stories to a crowd in the quad, or helping out a fellow student.

Zack is intelligent and offers a good balance to Jason's often gung-ho style. Though he's very courageous, he will also often as the voice of caution in unclear situations. Intuition is Zack's guide and he'll often act based on hunches and instincts.

As a Power Ranger, Zack draws his power from the Mastadon and his weapon is the Power Axe.

Weapon:
Power Axe

Zord:
Mastodon
Dinozord

Notes:
Zack developed his own special fighting style: Hip Hop Kido.

18

19

20

UH... MUST BE SOME SORT OF *SHORT*... I STILL HAVEN'T WORKED ALL THE *BUGS* OUT!

AN ARRIVING NEWS COPTER CAUGHT THIS TERRIFYING FOOTAGE FROM THE DIG SITE!

HEY, GUYS! THIS LOOKS *IMPORTANT!*

SO FAR THE GIANT SEEMS IMPERVIOUS TO ATTACK.

AUTHORITIES ARE CONCERNED IT MAY HEAD FOR THE CITY!

MONSTER ON RAMPAGE

WE'VE GOT TO GO!

GO? GO *WHERE?*

UH... YOU HEARD HIM! THAT THING MIGHT HEAD *HERE!*

SO WE'RE GOING TO... *HIDE!*

TURNING *TAIL*, EH?

29

ANYONE WITH A WEAPON THAT STILL WORKS, FIRE!

WHOOM

POW

ZAP

KABAMM

"ALL WE CAN DO NOW IS HOPE IT WORKED!"

LOOKS LIKE IT DID, BUT WHAT ABOUT THE DINOZORDS?!

I DON'T THINK THEY WERE DAMAGED. THAT RAY JUST MADE THEM SOMEHOW FALL APART! IF THAT'S TRUE, WE JUST HAVE TO PUT THEM BACK TOGETHER!

"JUST" HE SAYS.

WHAT'S UP WITH OUR HELMETS?!

THIS SURE IS A DIFFERENT LOOK!

HMM... MAYBE THAT RAY DISABLES MACHINERY BY SWITCHING PIECES WITH WHATEVER'S NEARBY! THE SAME COULD HAVE HAPPENED WITH OUR HELMETS.

FORTUNATELY, THE EFFECT DOESN'T SEEM TOO DANGEROUS!

HEY!

THE ANCIENT HEAD IS BROUGHT BEFORE THE DREADED **RITA REPULSA**, ALIEN SORCERESS BENT ON INTERGALACTIC DOMINATION!

AH HA HA HA HA HA HA HA! WELL DONE!

I CAN ALWAYS USE A NEW HEAD WHEN IT COMES TO DESTROYING THOSE MEWLING **RANGERS**!

AGES AGO, AFTER A BATTLE OF YEARS, SHE WAS DEFEATED BY **ZORDON** AND IMPRISONED ON THE MOON UNTIL RELEASED BY UNWITTING ASTRONAUTS!

I JUST HATE THEM SO MUCH! HA-HA-HA-HA!

NOW SHE AND HER MINIONS DWELL IN HER DARK PALACE ON THE **MOON**, PLOTTING TO CONQUER **EVERYTHING**, STARTING WITH THE **EARTH**!

YOU'RE THE SCIENTIST, **FINSTER**. WHAT DO YOU MAKE OF IT?

IT'S QUITE OLD, BUT IT **IS** A ROBOT! NOT AS SOPHISTICATED AS MY **OWN** MONSTERS, BUT **VERY** STRONG.

THE HEAD CONTAINS **BOTH** ITS INTELLIGENCE AND THAT INTERESTING **RAY** SQUATT TOLD US ABOUT!

WE DON'T UNDERSTAND A **THING** IT SAYS, BUT THAT RAY HAS ALREADY LEFT THE **RANGERS** HELPLESS!

SO, SQUATT, TELL ME, IF I HAVE FINSTER TAKE IT INTO HIS **MONSTER-MATIC** AND GIVE IT A **NEW** BODY, WILL IT **DESTROY** THE RANGERS FOR ME?

UH... IT ATTACKED THEM LAST TIME--

--AND HECK, **I'D** BE MAD IF SOMEONE KNOCKED **MY** HEAD OFF, SO I **GUESS** SO!

THEN, FINSTER, THE QUESTION ISN'T JUST WHAT YOU MAKE **OF** IT, BUT WHAT YOU CAN MAKE **OUT** OF IT!

GET IT?

HA HA HA HA HA HA!

37

45

51

ARE YOU **SURE** YOU CAN **REVERSE** THE RAY, ALPHA-5?

PRETTY **SURE!**

ALPHA-5, ARE YOU **ABSOLUTELY** SURE YOU DON'T WANT...

WE **COULD** JUST SWITCH HELMETS!

THEY WOULDN'T FIT! BESIDES THAT WOULDN'T HELP OUR **WEAPONS** OR THE **DINO-ZORDS!**

VRRRRRRRRRRRRRRRRRRRRRRRRRRRR

... **HELP?**

NO, DUDE! I **GOT** THIS!

ALPHA-5 DID IT! YOU'RE LOOKING TOTALLY **BLUE**, BILLY, BUT IN A **GOOD** WAY!

ISN'T ANYONE GOING TO SAY I'M IN THE **PINK?**

THE DINO-ZORDS ARE REASSEMBLING! HOW?

I THINK I UNDER-STAND!

THE ZORDS CAN'T **REPAIR** THEMSELVES, BUT THEY WEREN'T **DAMAGED**, JUST TAKEN APART!

WITHOUT THE NEGATIVE INFLUENCE OF THE RAY, THE PIECES ARE DRAWN BACK TOGETHER!

WHATEVER YOU SAY, BILLY!

AS LONG AS IT MEANS WE CAN KICK SOME **PUTTY!**

WATCH OUT FOR PAPERCUTZ™

Welcome to the first MIGHTY MORPHIN POWER RANGERS graphic novel, by Stefan Petrucha and PH Marcondes, from Papercutz, the perpetually-morphing comics company dedicated to publishing great graphic novels for all ages. I'm Jim Salicrup, the Editor-in-Chief, and I'm here to take you behind-the-scenes to explain exactly how this graphic novel came to be.

But first, I have to go into my rant. Once upon a time, comics (there really weren't any "graphic novels" back then) in North America were essentially for everyone. While generally considered kids' stuff, anyone could and would enjoy comics, no matter how old they were, or whether they were male or female. There was a comicbook for him or her. Now, things are a little different. Many comics and graphic novels are created for adults. Some, of course, are created just for children. But, if a comic or graphic novel declares itself suitable for all ages—well, folks think that just means kids. Which brings us to the MIGHTY MORPHIN POWER RANGERS.

Clearly, the original *Mighty Morphin Power Rangers* TV series was created for children. But those children who were fans of the original series are now adults, and many are into comics and graphic novels. When Papercutz first announced that we were launching a new series of POWER RANGERS graphic novels, the one question I got repeatedly was, "Which Power Rangers?" As PR fans all know, there have many incarnations of the Power Rangers over the past twenty years, the show keeps morphin into new series for new generations of fans. And whenever I answered an adult fan, and said we were publishing POWER RANGERS SUPER SAMURAI, they seemed to instantly lose interest, because that wasn't "their" Power Rangers. Always eager to please, I had to ask who were their Power Rangers, and the answer came back loud and clear—the MIGHTY MORPHIN POWER RANGERS! Countless fans would ask, and often demand, that we bring them back. And obviously, we did just that.

But as an Editor-in-Chief of a comics company, one of the things you wind up doing a lot is worry. In general, one of the biggest worries (and heartbreaks) is the fear of producing a wonderful graphic novel, with brilliant writing and awesome artwork, and no one finds out about it. And that was my concern with MIGHTY MORPHIN POWER RANGERS. Turns out, when we announced that we were bringing back MMPR at the San Diego Comic-Con, people paid attention! The Internet was suddenly all abuzz about the return of these classic super-heroes! Yet as we get closer and closer to our publication date, I'm still worried.

I'm worried that the fans that are most interested in this graphic novel, won't find us. If you're one of those fans, and you found us, I can't tell you how happy I am! I'm worried that this graphic novel will be shelved in the Children's Books sections in bookstores and the Kids Comics section in comicbook shops. Now, many people can't understand why that would worry me, after all, isn't MIGHTY MORPHIN POWER RANGERS a children's show? Well, yeah, over twenty years ago! Unless the original fans now have children of their own, how will they find us? One way we hope to direct comics fans to MIGHTY MORPHIN POWER RANGERS is by publishing a Free Comic Book Day comic featuring an all-new story, by our stellar creative team of Petrucha and Marcondes. (If you missed that, don't worry—we'll be collecting that story soon in an upcoming graphic novel!) Another way to bring attention to this series will be bringing on best-selling author, star of the TV series *Paranormal State*, and major MMPR fan Ryan Buell to co-write the next graphic novel along with Stefan.

Will it all work? Will the Mighty Morphin Power Ranger fans find us and enjoy what Stefan and PH (not to mention colorist, Laurie E. Smith, letterer, Bryan Senka, and Editor, Michael Petranek) created here? You tell us! Contact us through the means listed below, and let us know what you think! After all, if you didn't tell us you wanted the MIGHTY MORPHIN POWER RANGERS, this graphic novel simply wouldn't exist!

Go, go, POWER RANGERS!

Thanks,

JiM

STAY IN TOUCH!

FMAIL: salicrup@papercutz.com
WEB: www.papercutz.com
TWITTER: @papercutzgn
FACEBOOK: PAPERCUTZGRAPHICNOVELS
SNAIL MAIL: Papercutz, 160 Broadway, Suite 700, East Wing, New York, NY 10038

Mighty Morphin
A LOOK

It's Morphin Time!

Twenty years ago, an intergalactic being named Zordon ordered his friend and assistant, Alpha 5, to teleport five overbearing and overemotional humans (i.e. teenagers) to the Power Rangers Command Center and begin their journey as the first Power Rangers. August 28, 1993 marked an important date in television history with the first airing of *Mighty Morphin Power Rangers* on FOX. The show rapidly reached the hearts of children and became one of

Rita Repulsa and her crew in "Day of the Dumpster," the first episode of "Mighty Morphin Power Rangers"

the most popular live-action kid's series in the past two decades, with over 700 Power Rangers TV episodes having aired. The demographic spread from North America to more than 150 countries around the world with international airings of the shows, a live tour, two feature films (*Mighty Morphin Power Rangers: The Movie* and *Turbo: A Power Rangers Movie*), and countless products from a variety of licensees ranging from toys, video games, books, clothing, and household goods. The Power Rangers franchise was originally owned by Saban, bought by Disney, and then re-acquired by Saban Brands a few years ago.

Mighty Morphin Power Rangers was the beginning of a long line of Power Rangers. Each season followed the same concept of five chosen, good-hearted humans defending the planet Earth. The teenagers represent different cultures and nationalities but work together for the greater good. The original season taught great values to children through episodes and public service announcements.

Children and teenagers who watched the show in the first season are now adults who watch the show with their kids. I still remember watching the first episode, "Day of the Dumpster" with my little brother. We watched the episodes repeatedly and collected all of the toys. Now, I spread the love of the show with my two nephews (ages 2 and 6) and my kids (ages 1 and 3). Every time that I visit my nephews, they are running around the house with their Power Rangers Megaforce toys and cards. My daughter dressed as the Pink Megaforce Ranger for Halloween with great pride. I grew up watching Power Rangers while facing typical challenges in junior high school and high school. The show has always been a positive effect in my life and a major reason for becoming an active member in the online Power Rangers community.

Power Rangers is targeted for a young audience but has an extensive fanbase that spans to teenagers and adults. The

Power Rangers:
BACK

Movie Poster for "Mighty Morphin Power Rangers The Movie"

After Saban Brands re-purchased the Power Rangers brand, the Power Rangers name expanded with an official Twitter, Facebook, and Instagram.

Over 20 years after its debut, fans can watch every single episode of Power Rangers on Netflix. Shout!-Factory recently released the Power Rangers Legacy Collection, which has twenty years of Power Rangers episodes in a single DVD Set. Bandai America has released Power Rangers Action Card Game and Ranger Keys, featuring Rangers from the past 20 years. Bandai has also tailored to the collectors with the Power Rangers 20th Anniversary Legacy toyline. Mega Bloks released the Mighty Morphin Power Rangers 20th anniversary collector pack in late 2013.

The anniversary celebration continues with the 2014 Power Rangers Super Megaforce season. The Power Rangers will utilize their new Legendary Morphers and Ranger Keys to unlock the Powers of past Rangers. New and old fans will be able to watch twenty years of history as the Super Megaforce Rangers harness past weapons, Zords, and Megazords in addition to an explosive season finale with special Power Rangers guests. After 21 years, it appears that the Power Rangers franchise is just getting started!

first official Power Rangers convention took place in 2007 with two more following in 2010 and 2012. These conventions allow fans to interact with fellow fans and cast/crew members from the show. The Power Rangers online fandom has existed since the show began. Fans from all over the world are able to discuss the show and share their contributions through sites, blogs, and forums.

-Umesh Patel, Ranger Crew